J.C. HULSEY BOOKS

DYNAMITE

J.C. HULSEY

CHAPTER ONE

Wortham, Texas 1877

I saw her when she got off the 10 a.m. stage.

She was about five foot two, had curly brown hair, and was dressed in a light brown skirt with a thin, extra-tight, white blouse. Her boots looked a little out of place on such a pretty thing.

I wasn't the only one that saw her. That always happened when a pretty girl arrives. The men would stand around gawking, and the women would stick their noses in the air. I mopped my forehead with a dirty bandana, then stopped loading things and glanced at her again.

She finished giving the stage driver directions about her many suitcases and boxes, about twenty of them, then headed my way. "Is this your wagon?"

I just looked at her for a moment.

"Oh, I'm sorry. I thought you were in charge of it. I see you're wearing a badge, so can you tell me who owns this wagon?"

"The wagon belongs to me. I'm the temporary nighttime deputy. I just haven't taken the badge off this morning. What can I help you with?" I bent down and started fiddling with the harness.

"Is this wagon for hire? I need to get these boxes to Rolling Springs."

I remembered with a grin the last young girl I got involved with. She was a firecracker all right, and I had a feeling this brunette would be her match. I was now crowding forty, stood an even six feet, and had grayish hair and gray eyes.

I stopped messing with the harness and stood up straight, looking into her slate-blue eyes as she was standing on the platform above the street. "What is it you'd be wanting a rig like mine for?"

"As I stated, I have to take these boxes to my uncle in Rolling Springs. You do know where that is, don't you?"

"Now you done hurt my feelings. Of course I know where it is. I carry freight there all the time. What is it you got in them boxes?"

"I'll pay extra," she said, "if you don't concern yourself with what's in the cargo. Do you think you can handle that?"

"Depends on how much extra you're talking about."

"How does fifty dollars over your regular fee sound?"

"Move outta the way," I exclaimed, "so's I can git'em loaded."

They weren't all that heavy, so it made me wonder all the more what I was hauling. I set my load outa the wagon to make room for hers. I'd have to deliver it another time. I got all the boxes loaded, along with her luggage, and tied everything down.

"Climb aboard, and let's git moving."

She pulled herself up beside me on the wagon seat.

I had to admit that, even as an old cuss, I still admired the fairer sex, and she sure was a pretty little thing.

She settled onto the seat beside me.

"Get a good hold on somethin', it's gonna be a rough ride."

She gripped the sides of the seat and said, "I'm ready."

I slapped the reins, snapped my whip over the horse's heads, and we jerked as we headed out of town.

"How far is it to Rolling Springs?" she hollered over the noise of the wagon.

"Bout fifteen miles, give or take. We should get there close to midnight. You in a hurry?"

"Not really, I was just wondering. Are the roads always this rough?"

"Pretty much," I replied.

We rode a few more miles without either of us saying anything. I did, however, sneak glances at her. *'She sure is a good looking girl.'*

"Do you have any water? I could sure use a drink."

"Canteen in the back there. You want me to stop so's you can get it?"

"That won't be necessary. I'll just crawl over the seat and grab it."

"You ort not try that."

She started to stand up when the wagon hit a chuck hole and bounced her right onto my lap. I held onto her to keep her from falling out and almost lost control of the reins. When she scrambled to gain her balance, it only caused more trouble, so I pulled up on the reins and hollered for the team to stop. They finally came to a halt, and I helped her sit up straight.

"You shoulda waited for me to stop," I told her.

"I was sure I could climb over without any problem."

"Found out different, didn't you? Sometimes young folks need to listen to their elders."

"You're not that much older than me."

"Let's say I been down this road before and know how many potholes there is. Just how old are you, and how old do you think I am?" I asked.

"I'm almost twenty-six, and I'd say that you're about thirty five . . . maybe less."

"Alright, you've made your point. Ain't you gonna have a drink while we're stopped?"

"I forgot."

"Must not'a been thirsty."

"Can you get it for me?"

I grabbed the canteen and handed it to her. When she pulled the cork out of the top and turned it up, I watched her beautiful throat swallow.

I slapped the reins against the horse's rump. When the wagon jerked, the water sloshed out onto her.

"You could have warned me," she huffed.

"You was the one said you was ready."

She pushed the cork back into the canteen and tossed it in the back.

"You orta take it easy with that. It's our only supply of water."

"Why is it our only supply?"

"Wasn't planning on having a passenger, but here you are. Amazing how things change so quick like." I looked at her curiously. "You ready to tell me what we're carrying?"

"Why is it so important for you to know?"

"Well, if it was nitroglycerin, then I would take another route, and if it was whiskey, I'd stop for a drink any time. Why is it you don't want to tell me?"

"Alright. If you must know, it's dynamite."

"Dynamite! Why in blazes didn't you tell me that when we started?"

"If you had known, would you have agreed to carry it?"

"Probably not."

"That's why I didn't tell you. Are you going to turn back now?"

"Too late for that, we're over halfway there. What's your uncle gonna do with all them explosives?"

"He's building a fence and has a lot of stumps and rocks to move out of the way."

"Pretty drastic way of doing things. Sure hope he knows how to handle the stuff."

"I'm sure he does. He was in the war, you know. He handled explosives there."

"I reckon he knows then."

By the way I'm Jubal Foxworth."

"And my name is Ruby Cantrell."

"Your uncle is Bertrem Cantrell?" I asked. "His place is a few miles this side of Rolling Springs."

"Yes, he's my uncle. Why?"

"Me and old man Cantrell don't get along."

"Why is that?"

"A few years back he sold me a horse."

"Well, he does own a horse ranch."

"Yeah, and him owning a horse ranch, he shoulda known that horse was gonna go lame two days after I rode him away."

"He can't know something like that," she exclaimed. "You expected him to predict the future?"

"I still say he shoulda known."

"You said you're Jubal Foxworth? I've heard of you. You're famous. Ned Buntline wrote about you. You're some kind of fast gun or something."

"Ain't nothing but a passel of lies."

"You mean he didn't tell the truth about you?"

"Let's just say he exaggerated a might."

"Why would he do something like that?"

"Why do most people do things? For money. Look at me, I probably wouldn't have taken this job if you hadn't offered more money."

"How much of the stories are exaggerated?"

"Why don't we talk about something else?"

"What would you like to talk about?"

"How come a pretty girl like you is delivering dynamite? Why didn't old Bertrem send one of his hands to pick it up?"

"If you must know, his neighbor isn't too happy about him fencing his property, so we thought if his niece came for a visit, no one would think anything was out of place."

"Has there been any trouble with old man Renfro? I mean bad trouble?"

"There have been a lot of threats, but nothing more. At least that's what uncle Bernie has told me."

"If Renfro finds out about this dynamite, you can bet there'll be more than threats."

"If any of those stories about you are true, then you could help Uncle Bernie, couldn't you?"

"I gave up that life a long time ago."

"But what if I asked you to help?"

"Depends. What're you offering?"

"Well, I know how much you like money, so what if I said I would offer a sufficient amount for the job?"

He said, "What if I wanted something other than money?"

"And, pray tell, what would be better than money?"

"I've always been fond of pretty girls."

"You're not suggesting that I . . . "

"I'm not suggesting anything. I'm telling you that's what it'll take."

"You can't be serious!" she huffed.

"This is a serious matter."

"I'm going to have to give it a lot of thought," she said. "Maybe we won't need your help after all."

CHAPTER TWO

I looked at the darkening clouds ahead. We were in for some heavy rain. I pulled up on the reins and hollered for the team to stop.

"What are we stopping for?"

"Take a look at those clouds. It's gonna be raining any minute now. There's slickers in the back of the wagon."

I crawled down, walked to the back, and retrieved a couple of ponchos. When I got back, I handed her one.

"This is filthy. I can't wear this."

"I'd put it on and be quick about it, if you don't want to get soaked."

As the rain started coming down, she reluctantly pulled it over her head. Big pelts of rain were making it extremely hard to see the road. "I think we'd better find some shelter until this blows over. There's a line shack a few yards off the main road. Belongs to Renfro. I don't reckon he'll mind us using it to get outta the rain. We can also eat a little something."

I pulled up in front of the shack, set the brake, and tied the reins around the handle. "Better git inside before it gits worse."

She climbed down and ran for the shack, and I watched as she pushed on the door. She was having a hard time getting it open.

After grabbing my bedroll and a sack of grub that I always carried with me, I went to help her.

"It seems to be locked."

"Nobody never locks a line shack. Move outta the way."

I pushed with my shoulder and it popped open.

"You ain't got enough meat on your bones for a job like that."

"It was pretty hard to open. I saw you straining a little yourself. Don't deny it."

"Alright, I admit it was stuck pretty good. Come on in and close it."

She stepped inside and pulled the door closed behind her. "This is dreadful. It's so dark, I can hardly see."

"At least we're outta the rain. Better than getting soaked, ain't it?" I asked.

"I suppose."

We were both already drenched and, when she removed the slicker, her paper-thin blouse was clinging to her, giving the appearance she wasn't wearing anything.

I lit a little lamp I found on the homemade table, and it caused a halo of light around the room. Then I laid my bedroll out and set the sack beside it.

"What's the bedroll for? Surely we're not going to spend the night here?"

"Depends on Mother Nature, now don't it. If it was still daylight maybe we could go on, but if I can't see the road I might run in a ditch, and that wouldn't be good, seeing as we're carrying dynamite. You can understand that, can't you? See that cot in the corner over there?" I pointed at a dusty cot on the other side of the room.

"Is that what you call it? I imagine it's filthy and full of all kind of insects."

"That's what the bedroll is for. Ain't no bugs in it. At least I don't think there is."

"But there's only one bedroll. Where are you going to sleep?"

"You remember me telling you how I'm fond of pretty girls."

"Do you remember I said we probably wouldn't need your help?"

"At least you're not saying no. I'm gonna eat a couple pieces of jerky and have a drink of whiskey, and then try to get some sleep. You want some?"

"I don't normally drink whiskey, but I do have a chill. Sure, I'll have a small one, and a piece of jerky if that's all you have."

I handed her a small piece of jerky and the bottle. She laid the jerky on the table and twisted the lid off the bottle, then turned it up and took a big swallow. She sputtered and spewed. I could tell she wasn't used to drinking.

"That was good. Here." She coughed and handed it to me.

I chug-a-lugged and handed it back to her, then she slugged down another one.

~~~~~~~~~~~~~~~~

The morning dawned with a bright sun shining through the window. Ruby held her hand in front of her face in an attempt to shade her eyes. It wasn't keeping the sun out the way she had planned. The room was so bright it was almost blinding. *'Perhaps,'* she thought, *'if I hadn't drank so much whiskey, I wouldn't have this awful headache.'* She lay back down pulling the cover over her head.

'Maybe in a few minutes I can face the day. What exactly did happen last night? I remember Jubal telling me how pretty he thought I was, then he opened that bottle of rotgut. I should have known better, but I didn't want to hurt his feelings by refusing. What difference does it make if I hurt his feelings or not? It's not like he means anything to me. Wait a cotton-picking minute. I'm not wearing any clothes. What did happen?'

She looked around for Jubal, but he wasn't in the room. She struggled out of bed and got dressed, wishing again she hadn't had all that whiskey. *'Maybe some*
~~~~~~~~~~~~~~~~

bacon and eggs will make me feel better, but you ain't got no bacon and eggs. Oh. My aching head. You're an idiot, Ruby Cantrell.'

She noticed a bucket of water sitting on the table. She walked over to it and splashed her face with the cool liquid, then drank a big dipper full.

She saw Jubal's sack sitting by the door where he had dropped it. She began rummaging in it, searching for something to eat, and maybe something for her head. She didn't find anything for her head, but lo and behold there was a small slab of bacon, coffee, a pot and other things.

"Now if I only had a couple of eggs," as she filled a pot with water for coffee. She, then sat in one of the chairs and put her face in her hands. "Oh, my aching head."

Just about then, Jubal came in the door holding his hat in his hands.

"Found some guineas wandering around, so I followed them to their nest and got us some eggs," I said. "Say, you don't look so good. Got a headache, do you?"

"I was just now wishing I had some bacon and eggs. Maybe that would make me feel better. What are guineas?"

"They're a little like chickens, but a bit wilder. What matters is we got eggs. If you want, I can tell you how to help your hangover."

"Okay, what do I do?" she asked in defeat.

I smiled, knowing how this was going to sound. "Fill a cup half full with whiskey, then break one of these eggs in it. Drink it down in one gulp, and I guarantee you will feel better."

"I believe I've had enough whiskey to last me a lifetime."

"Suit yourself, but I recommend it highly."

"Okay, but if it doesn't work, you're going to be in a lot of trouble."

"That won't be anything new for me."

"Would you mind handing me the bottle?" she asked.

I handed it to her and she poured the whiskey in.

"Now, if you would hand me one of the eggs."

I handed her an egg, but her hand was shaking so much I took it back. "Let me do it for you?" I broke it in the cup and swished it around. "Now drink it straight down."

I held her hands so she wouldn't spill it, and she put it to her lips.

"It smells awful. I can't drink this."

"Hold your nose and chug a lug it the way you did the whiskey last night."

"Oh, please don't say that word."

I helped her again as she held her nose, and we got it all down her.

"Oh! That's bad stuff. You guaranteed it to work, right?"

"Give it a little time. It will work. You want me to fix the eggs?"

"You cook?" She looked surprised.

"I think I can manage, if you don't feel up to it."

Let me sit for a couple of minutes. Why did you give me all that whiskey?"

"Hey, I didn't twist your arm. You could have quit after the first one, so don't blame me."

"I guess I'm mad at myself more than you," she said, standing up. "Give me the eggs. Fried or scrambled?"

"Scrambled is good," I said. "I'm real sorry you've got a hangover. Let me slice the bacon, and fry a few extra to eat on the way." I noticed the full pot on the counter. "I see you made coffee."

"Yeah, but where'd the water come from?" she asked.

"Rain water. It did rain, remember?" I teased.

She ignored the remark. "Was it hard finding the eggs? You said you had to chase the guineas."

"Yeah. Them little rascals are plenty fast. They would take off one direction, then all of a sudden, they were going another. I fell on my face more than a couple times, but I was finally rewarded with these beauties." I handed my hat to her.

When she smiled it brightened the whole room.

"You should do that more often."

"Do what?"

"Smile."

"Was I smiling?"

"You were."

"I didn't realize. I sure don't feel like smiling."

"What did I do or say to make you smile?"

"I don't remember, but it must have been something funny." She looked up at me like something sparked in her mind. "I remember now. You were telling me about running behind those guineas. I can just picture you chasing them around," she said as she removed the bacon and broke the eggs into the skillet.

"I reckon it was funny, since it wasn't you doing the chasing. Speaking of eggs, those about ready?"

"Sit down and I'll dish them up. How come you carry bacon with you?"

"Ain't you glad I do? Can never tell when something like a rain storm's gonna chase me under cover. It's nice to have something to eat if it happens."

"I haven't eaten guinea eggs before."

"There're pretty much the same as chicken eggs. Dig in, you'll see."

She lifted a small spoon full to her lips, then hesitated.

"Go ahead, you're a big girl. You should be able to do this."

She put it into her mouth and chewed. "They taste just like regular eggs. You want that other piece of bacon?" she asked, then poured herself another cup of coffee.

"Help yourself. By the way, the reason the eggs taste so good is you're a good cook. How's the headache?"

"I do believe it's a little better. And anybody can scramble eggs." Now that breakfast is over, I think we need to talk."

"What about?"

"You really don't have any idea, do you?"

"You mean last night?"

"Yes. I mean last night. What happened? Did we. . .?"

"You don't remember?"

"If I did, I wouldn't have to ask, now would I?"

"Well, we had a few drinks."

"I know that much. When I woke up this morning, I didn't have any clothes on. Where did you sleep? Did we? Will you tell me already?"

"Nothing happened. Your virtue is still intact. You were feeling pretty good. You stripped off all your clothes and invited me to come to bed with you, but I like my women to be clear headed and know what they're doing. So, I put you to bed right before you passed out."

"But you said you wanted. I mean you hinted that you liked pretty girls. If I offered, why did you turn me down?" I had the feeling she was a little disappointed.

"Like I said, I prefer you be sober when you offer yourself to me."

"I don't think you'll have to worry about that happening again."

"Oh it'll happen and next time you'll be sober."

"You're awfully sure of yourself," I noticed her body quiver as if a chill had come through the room.

"Yep, I'm sure."

She turned away and began clearing the table.

"We should probably get back on the road. We're getting a late start as it is. Your uncle is probably wondering if something happened to you."

"Uncle Bernie knows I'm a big girl."

"I'll go get the team ready. Why don't you clean up the place a bit?"

I headed out the door when she said something so quiet, I almost didn't hear.

"Thank you."

I turned in the doorway and asked, "For what?"

"For not taking advantage of me when I had too much to drink."

"The only reason I didn't, Ruby Cantrell, is because I like you. A lot."

I turned and went out the door, not waiting for her to reply. *Yes, Ruby Cantrell, you're special, mighty special.*

I got the team ready to go and went back inside. "You 'bout ready?"

"I'm going to miss this little shack."

"We could stay another night," I said.

"I don't think so. I'm ready."

I grabbed my bed roll, which she had ready, and the sack of grub. "Let's go." *'Dang if I wasn't gonna miss this place, too.'*

Nothing was said for a few miles. It was slow going, and the mud was straining the team. Ruby was holding on to the side of the seat, but was still being bounced against me.

"Have you given any more thought to helping Uncle Bernie?" she asked.

"If I decide to help, I'd be doing it for you, not him."

"I guess it wouldn't matter, as long as you're there."

"What's the reason Cantrell wants to fence his land?"

"I don't know exactly why, but he said something about Renfro's cattle drifting onto his land. He says there is only enough grass for his horses."

"I thought the majority of it was open range. He can't fence that."

"He said there's an unwritten law that the first one to use the land for ten years has a right to claim it as his."

"But they got here about the same time."

"Yes, but Uncle Bernie had horses on it almost four years before Renfro started driving cattle on it."

"I can understand why Renfro is mad. Cantrell's property has the best grass and water. Has he tried talking to Renfro?"

"I don't know the whole story. You're going to have to get Uncle Bernie to explain everything to you. How much further?"

"About four or five miles. It's taking longer because of all this mud. You anxious to see him?"

"I haven't seen him for almost a year. He came to visit when he was buying cattle, then six months later when my parents died."

"How did they die?"

"They were on their way back from the county picnic when a wheel came off their buggy. It overturned, and they were both killed instantly. When Uncle Bernie sent the letter asking me to visit, I was glad to have a place to go. I was packed and ready to leave when I received a telegram asking me to bring the dynamite, so I told him I would."

"I still think he should have sent one of his hands to pick it up. What would you do if you ran into trouble?"

"I feel sure you would protect me."

"What would you have done if I'd turned you down?"

"I'm sure someone in town would have been willing to help a poor, defenseless girl deliver some boxes to her uncle."

"There's the gate up ahead," I said.

"Where's the house?"

"It's still a half mile. The Rocking C Ranch is one of the largest in the county."

"Why does one person need so much land?"

"For grass, for water, because they're greedy," I said, thinking of how I felt about her uncle.

"I don't think Uncle Bernie is greedy."

"Maybe, maybe not. I only know I don't like him or trust him."

"Maybe if you explained to him how you felt, the two of you could work out some sort of agreement. I've always believed him to be honest and fair."

"There's the main house up ahead there."

"Why, it's huge. Somehow, I thought it would be more like . . . well, more like that shack where we spent the night."

"Why would you think that?"

"I don't really know why. I had pictured in my head a bunch of cowboys driving cattle on the trail, and then sitting around a campfire drinking coffee. I can't picture any of them living in a place like this."

"You're right about most cowboys. They don't have much, but the owners . . . well, the majority of them, live mighty well."

"There's Uncle Bernie waiting for us."

Bernie Cantrell hadn't changed a bit. Perhaps his brown hair was a bit grayer and he was a size larger, but he was still dressed in blue dungarees and blue chambray shirt, and sporting that famous ten-gallon hat that he always wore. He was standing on one of the few dry spots in the yard.

"I don't figure he's waiting for us, just you."

"Please be nice. He will be."

"We'll see."

I pulled the wagon to a halt in front of Bernie Cantrell, then set the brake and tied the reins around the handle. I'm not afraid of anything or anybody, but at this moment, my guts were tied in a knot.

Ruby jumped down, ignoring the puddles of water, and ran into Cantrell's arms.

"Ruby! I'm glad you're here. I was getting a little worried when you didn't show up yesterday."

"We had to stop because of the storm, so we spent the night in Renfro's line shack," she said.

"You got the dynamite?" he asked her, though he was looking hard at me.

"It's in the wagon," Ruby said. "Are you going to say hello to your old friend?"

"Jubal Foxworth ain't no friend of mine. Couldn't you find nobody else to bring you out here?" Cantrell asked.

"Uncle Bernie! Jubal—I mean Mr., Foxworth—did both of us a favor by bringing me and the dynamite here safely. You could at least be civil to him."

"Howdy, Foxworth," he said. "Thanks for watching over Ruby."

"Glad to do it. Ruby also invited me to sign on. Said something about you having some trouble with Renfro."

"I don't need help from the likes of you," he huffed. "If you'll pull your rig over to the barn, I'll have a couple of the boys unload and you can head back to town."

"Sure thing, Mr. Cantrell," I snarled at him. I pulled the wagon over to the barn.

Cantrell's foreman and another hand started unloading the boxes and stacking them in the barn.

I glanced back at Cantrell and Ruby. She was talking up a storm and waving her hands around like a windmill. He would start to say something, and she would begin again. He shook his head, then turned and starting walking toward the barn.

"Ned," he said to the older man, "you and Drew take Miss Cantrell's suitcases in the house when you're finished unloading the boxes."

"Yes sir, Boss," said Ned.

"Foxworth?" he started, "it seems you made quite an impression on Ruby. If she feels that strongly about you, then maybe I'd be willing to consider hiring you. Just until this mess is cleared up."

"If I decide to stay, you and me need to sit down and have a pow wow. I've still got some hard feelings about that horse you sold me."

"Why, it's been a few years since that happened," he said. "If you had come to me back then and told me, I would have let you have your pick of any horse on the ranch. But you didn't do that, you just kept it to yourself and let it fester all this time? We was good friends until then. You started turning and walking the other way when I would see you in town."

"So, you're telling me I could have brought that lame horse back and you would have given me another?"

"That's what I'm telling you. You think maybe we could shake on it and be friends again?"

"I reckon that sounds like a good idea." I grasped his hand and we shook, like two old friends.

"Now, explain to me why you spent the night alone in Renfro's line shack with my niece," he said in a hushed tone.

"The storm got so bad I couldn't see the road, so we stopped at the shack instead of taking a chance on running off the road with that precious cargo of yours."

"Where did you sleep?" he demanded. "If I remember correctly, there ain't but one bunk in that shack."

"Nothing happened, if that's what you're asking. Ruby is still as pure as she was when she stepped off that stage."

"I'll be talking to her about this," he said.

"Now, how 'bout you filling me in on what the trouble is?" I asked him.

"Come on in the house. We'll have a drink and I'll tell you everything."

"What about my wagon? You want me to put it anyplace in particular?"

"Just leave it for now. I'll get one of the boys to put it back of the barn and unhitch the team."

Ruby came to meet us as we headed to the main house. "You two get everything worked out?" she asked.

"Yep!" we said at the same time.

She pushed her way between the two of us, linking her arms in ours. She had an even bigger grin on her face than she'd had back in the shack. She was absolutely glowing. *Yes, Ruby Cantrell, you are a very special young woman.*

Bernie opened the front door and motioned Ruby and me in.

"Sandra," he yelled. "We have guests. Bring some snacks into the parlor."

"Yes sir, Mr. Cantrell," a middle-aged woman with a Mexican accent answered.

We followed Bernie into a very spacious room. Leather-covered furniture adorned the place, and paintings covered the walls. A large rock fireplace stretched across the far wall, and a big portrait of Bernie was hanging above the mantle.

"Kind of full of yourself, ain't you?" I asked Bernie, indicating the painting.

"That was done while my Mildred was still alive at her request. It does look kind of nice hanging there, don't you think?"

"It looks lovely, Uncle Bernie," said Ruby.

"Thank you, my dear. I've got the map on my desk, Jubal. Come on over here and I'll try to explain to you where I think Renfro's gonna cause trouble." He unrolled a map on the desk. "It's right where his property loops back into mine. See how this little creek hooks back? I mean, that's where I would do it."

"What you gonna do if he starts shooting?"

"I learned a long time ago that, if somebody shoots at you, you better shoot back and be a better shot."

"Have you tried talking to him?"

"Of course. I've been over to his place at least three times. Last time he got so mad I thought he was gonna fight me."

"So talking ain't gitting it done. Have you offered money? I've found that money smooths out a lot of problems."

"No, I didn't offer money. I don't feel like I should have to pay for what's already mine."

"Wouldn't a little payoff beat somebody getting killed?"

"Since you put it that way, I reckon it would be better. You wanna ride over there with me in the morning so I can make an offer."

"I guess I can do that. Where 'bouts you want me to sleep? In the bunkhouse?"

"Since we're gonna be leaving at first light, you can sleep upstairs. There are plenty of rooms. Sandra has a room off the kitchen, and I have a bedroom downstairs. I'm getting too old to keep climbing those blasted stairs."

Ruby, you've been sitting there not saying anything. What do you think about all this?" I asked her.

"I don't have an opinion. I don't know enough about it. When I do, I'll say something."

"Dinner is served," said the cook.

"Good, I'm famished," Bernie said. "I had Sandra wait, hoping you would show up today. She's a fine cook. You won't find a better one in all of Rafter County."

"I don't know about that, Bernie. Ruby is a fair cook, in a bind," I told him.

"Where did the two of you spend the night, Ruby?" he asked.

"I told you, in Renfro's line shack," she answered. "I didn't figure he'd deny shelter to get out of the storm."

"He might, since we're having this disagreement. Just sit anywhere, we don't hold with formalities here."

"Uncle Bernie, have you ever eaten guinea eggs?"

"Only in a pinch, and only if I can catch them. Those rascals can run faster than a jackrabbit. Their eggs have a wild taste to them that I don't care for. Why do you ask?"

"That's what we had for breakfast. Jubal chased down a pack of them and persuaded them to give up half a dozen. I thought they tasted just like chicken eggs."

"Maybe you were just hungry. You know everything tastes better when you're hungry."

"Dig in. We don't have any guinea eggs, but we've got a fine meal here," the cook said.

The meal was very good, but I kept thinking of those eggs Ruby fixed that morning. *Ruby Cantrell, you're a special girl.*

When we were finished eating, Bernie asked me, "Is there anything more we need to discuss?"

"No, I think we pretty much covered everything. I think I'll go outside and look around a little, if it's okay with you?

"Sure, maybe Ruby wants to go with you. It's been a while since she's been here, but she can show you what she remembers," Bernie suggested.

"You want to show me around?" I asked her.

"Sure. I don't know how much I'll be able to show, but I'll try."

We told Bernie we'd be back in an hour or so and left the house.

"Looks like the ground is drying pretty good," I said.

"Yes, it is," she said. "Listen, if Uncle Bernie asks about last night anymore, you don't have to tell him everything."

"There's isn't anything to tell, other than you woke up naked as a jaybird," I teased.

"Oh, you!" She hit me on the shoulder.

"I figure what goes on between you and me stays between you and me, don't you agree?" I asked.

"I believe that's a really good idea."

"Let's take a walk out to the little corral behind the barn," she said. "That's where he keeps the best stock."

She slipped her arm through mine, and I had to follow her as she led the way.

"There it is, and look at that Black Stallion. Isn't he beautiful? Uncle Bernie breeds some of the best horses in the country."

"He is a beauty alright. I wish I made enough money to buy a horse like that."

"Maybe someday you will."

"Not hauling freight, I won't."

"Isn't that a beautiful sunset?" She pointed at the horizon. The golden glow of the setting sun was casting yellow and red streaks of light in the barnyard. It was a pretty sight, but even its beauty didn't compare to that of the girl standing next to me.

'What's the matter with you, Foxworth—thinking all this mushy stuff? Though she is prettier than the sunset.'

We continued talking and kidding with one another as we walked back to the house.

Bernie was waiting for us and asked, "You want a drink before you turn in?"

"Sure, I'll have a small one. You want one Ruby?" I asked her.

"I think I'll pass and go on up to bed." She gave me the evil eye for suggesting she have a drink. "Goodnight, Uncle Bernie. Goodnight, Jubal."

"Goodnight," we said in unison.

I watched her as she started up the stairs. What a sight for an old man's eyes.

"Jubal? Jubal?"

"What? Oh, did you say something, Bernie?"

"Where was your mind just then?"

"Someplace it shouldn't have been, I imagine. What were you saying?"

He was pouring whiskey in a glass. "I was going over the plan for tomorrow. I wanted your input about it, but I guess you must be tired. I don't reckon you want that drink after all? We can go over the plan in the morning on the way there. How's that sound?"

"Sounds like a good idea. I believe I'll turn in now. I was up pretty early chasing those guineas. Which room do you want me in?"

"Any of them. I have a room downstairs. Oh, you better check which one Ruby is in. I wouldn't want you to go in her room by mistake."

'It wouldn't be no mistake if I went in her room. I thought to myself.'

"Goodnight, Bernie. I'm glad we got everything worked out between us."

"I'm glad too. Goodnight, see you in the morning. Say, Jubal?"

"Yeah."

"Do you need to check in with the sheriff? You being his deputy and all," he asked.

"No, he knows it's just temporary for me."

CHAPTER THREE

I walked up the stairs and knocked softly on the first door.

"Yes? Who is it?" Ruby asked.

I turned the knob and stepped inside.

"I don't think I said come in, but since you're here, we should talk."

"I don't think you really want to talk, do you?" I walked toward her.

"What are you doing?"

I didn't answer, just took her in my arms and kissed her. She kissed back. *Maybe she does like me,* I thought.

I released her lips and leaned back so I could look into those slate-blue eyes of hers. They were like magical pools of clear water that seemed to know what I was thinking. "That kiss tells me that you like me just a little."

"Of course I like you. After all, you're doing us a big favor by offering to help."

"That wasn't a helping us kiss," I said. "I told Bernie, and now I'm telling you, the only reason I'm helping is because of you."

"I hope you aren't expecting anything in return."

"I wouldn't turn it down if it was offered," I said.

"You already turned down an offer. At least that's what you told me."

"I explained how come I did that. And I told you before that I'm partial to pretty girls."

"So, you think I'm pretty?"

"One of the prettiest I've ever seen. I think you're very special."

"Why do you think that?"

"I suppose it's the way you affect me. I've known my share of women, but none of them have made me feel the way you do."

"You affect me the same way," she said. "I don't mean I've known a lot of men, but there is something about you that I just can't explain."

She pulled my head down and pressed her lips to mine. It was a deep soul-satisfying kiss that just about knocked my socks off. An involuntary groan came from me. *'Ruby Cantrell, you are very special.'*

We continued kissing. Then she pushed me away.

"Just because we're kissing doesn't mean anything else is going to happen."

"Of course not. Why would I think that?" I captured her lips again and this time it was her that moaned.

She pushed me back again and said, "We better stop now while we still can. When or if it does happen, I don't want it to be a hasty, rushed thing. I, like most women, would prefer a little romance."

"You mean like candy and flowers? Stuff like that?"

"What was it you said a moment ago? I wouldn't turn it down if it was offered."

"I wasn't talking about flowers or candy." I said. "What's your favorite flower and candy?"

"You're serious, aren't you?"

"If that's what it's gonna take to get this done, then yeah, I'm serious, dead serious."

"I don't really have a favorite flower or candy. Anything would be fine, as long as it's given sincerely."

"Darling, I can't be any more sincere. As I have said, Ruby Cantrell, you're very special."

"That's sweet, but now I think you should go to your own room."

"What would you say if I told you I don't have a room?"

"I'd say you better find one because you aren't staying in this one. Not tonight."

"That sounds like there might be hope for another night."

"We'll just have to wait and see. Goodnight, Mr. Foxworth." She shoved me toward the door.

I went reluctantly, turning in the doorway, looking downhearted.

"Goodnight," she said a little too loudly.

I closed the door and went into the next room. Once inside, I reflected on what had just happened.

'What is it about this young woman that has a hold on me? She's not all that good looking—wait, what am I saying? She's gorgeous . . . and her lips? Have I ever tasted anything as sweet or felt anything as soft as her lips? Is she the one? I've always run the other way when a girl wanted to get too serious, but here I am wishing she would get serious about me.'

I splashed some water on my face, got undressed, and climbed into bed. I closed my eyes, and the next thing I knew it was morning. I had dreamt only of Ruby Cantrell. First of a young Ruby like she is now, then an older Ruby with half a dozen kids hanging on her skirt waiting for me to get home, and finally an even older Ruby, after the kids were grown and gone, sitting in a rocking chair looking across the room at . . . who was she looking at? I couldn't see clearly enough.

I got out of bed and splashed a little water on my face, then got dressed. I went into the hallway and knocked on Ruby's door, but there was no answer. I twisted the doorknob and stuck my head inside, and the room was empty.

As I was walking down the stairs, I overheard Bernie and Ruby talking at the table.

"I'm just saying, can I really trust him to be on my side if push comes to shove?" Bernie asked.

"He's a very special individual. I would trust him with my life, if that tells you anything," Ruby said emphatically.

"How can you judge him so quickly? You've only known him a couple of days, but I've known him for a few years. In all that time, I've never known him to pick sides. He's always been sort of a loner."

"All I can say is I like him. A lot. And he's agreed to help you with this problem, so I don't think you should look a gift horse in the mouth. As the owner of a horse ranch, you should know and accept that."

"Harrumph," I cleared my throat noisily as I entered the dining room. "Good morning, folks."

"Good morning to you, Jubal," Bernie said.

"Good morning, Jubal," Ruby said. "Did you sleep well?"

"I did. Had a lot of dreams that didn't make sense, but other than that I slept very well."

"Have a seat, there's plenty to eat. Sandra made extra because you and Ruby are here. Of course, if there's something you'd rather have, speak up," Bernie said.

"You wouldn't happen to have any guinea eggs, would you?" I glanced at Ruby and she seemed to swallow something the wrong way.

"Are you alright, Ruby?" asked a concerned Bernie.

"I'm fine, Uncle Bernie. Thanks for asking. I just got something in my windpipe."

"Try chewing slower," Bernie said. "You 'bout ready to go, Jubal?"

CHAPTER FOUR

"Ready as I'll ever be, but I don't have a saddle horse. My team ain't broke for the saddle," I told him.

"I reckon we can scare up a mount for you," Bernie said.

"Okay, then let's go. You bringing some money with you?" I asked.

"Don't figure I'll need it, but yes, I've got some."

"This ain't gonna work unless you put some effort into it. You should at least act like you're wanting to settle this peaceably."

"You're right, I know, but I also know Renfro. I've talked and talked until I was tired of talking. He can be one cantankerous old bastard."

"Even cantankerous old bastards like money. Just give it a try."

"I sure hope you're right."

We rode the rest of the way in silence, each of us thinking about what we were going to do if this meeting turned sour. *'I suppose that's the reason for my being here. If there is any gunplay, I am supposed to defuse it, however I can.*

I thought I was done with that kind of life, but here I am, fixing to step in the middle of something that could get me dead. All because of a pretty girl.'

A little after noon we were met at Renfro's gate by his foreman and two drovers . . . at least I thought they were drovers. On second glance, I realized I'd never seen drovers with tied down guns like these two were sporting.

"What do you want here, Cantrell?" asked the foreman, a big-boned, thin man with brown, leathery skin, who was wearing typical cowboy garb. The other two were dressed the same, except for their pistols.

"We want to talk to Renfro," Bernie answered.

"What's Foxworth doing with you? I understood the two of you was on the outs."

"I don't see as how that's any concern of yours. Are you gonna let us talk to your boss?"

"Drop in behind me and I'll take you to him. You two stay here and don't let anybody else in."

We followed him to the main house almost a mile from the gate.

"Why don't you wait here while I check and see if he wants to see you?" He got off his horse and walked through the iron gate and into the house.

A few minutes passed, then the door slammed open and a large round-bellied man came storming out. He stood approximately five foot five, and weighed about 200 pounds. He was dressed awfully fancy for a working cowboy, and he looked to be close to sixty years old.

"Cantrell! I thought I heard enough of your spiel last time you wus here. What else do you have to say? And what is Foxworth doing here with you? I thought . . . "

"Never mind about him. This is between you and me?"

"I figure you included him when you rode onto my property with him. Speak your peace and make this the last time. I don't want you to keep coming around unless you're willing to stop fencing my property."

"It ain't your prop—"

Bernie was getting agitated, so I cut him off and said, "Bernie, make him an offer."

"Alright, Renfro, here's the deal. I'm willing to compensate you for agreeing to step back and not fuss about me fencing my property."

"And just what kind of compensation are you suggesting?" roared Renfro.

"How's $25,000 sound?" asked Bernie.

"That's quite a chunk of change. How come you're willing to do this?" Renfro asked.

"To be honest, it was Foxworth's idea. He figured some money might be better than scattering bodies across the prairie. So, what'd you say?" asked Bernie.

"Like I said, $25,000 is an awful lot of money, but it ain't enough. I've told you more than once, that property is as much mine as yours. By damn, if it takes a few dead bodies to convince you, then so be it. Now, you and your friend go back the way you came. And don't let your shirttail hit your back."

We turned our horses and headed back down the trail.

"Don't come back," Renfro shouted. "You're not welcome here!"

"I knew it wouldn't work. He's too hardheaded for his own good," exclaimed Bernie.

"You wouldn't know that if you hadn't tried. Now we need to come up with a strategy so nobody gits killed."

"I sure hope you got some ideas, 'cause I sure don't."

We passed through the gate where the two cowboy/gunfighters were standing guard. I nodded to them and they nodded back, both still with their hands on their weapons. They were ready anytime, and they could see I was too.

"Looks like Renfro's already hired some guns," I said to Bernie.

"Those two? They're just a couple of drovers. I seen 'em in town with Renfro a couple of times."

"Were they wearing their guns when you saw them?"

"Come to think of it, when they were in town, no, they weren't. And today they did look like they were well acquainted with the hardware they were wearing. I guess Renfro's gittin' more serious than I thought."

"Let's git on home and figure something out. Is your cook gonna fix a swell supper like the breakfast? You do realize we missed dinner?"

"A cowboy misses lots of meals. I told you she was the best cook in the county, didn't I?"

"That you did. That you did."

"Come on, we don't want to upset her by being too late," Bernie said as he spurred his horse into a gallop.

I followed on my new horse, and we rode our mounts directly into the barn where two of Bernie's hands were pitching hay into the loft.

"Ned, you and Drew take care of our horses, will you?" Bernie said to the men.

"Sure, Boss. If I can ask, did things go okay with old man Renfro?" the younger of the two asked.

"I don't want you boys to concern yourself with that kind of stuff. You just keep doing what you've been doing."

"If gunplay happens here at the ranch, then I figure we'll need to get involved, ain't that the case?" the older cowboy asked.

"Ned, I reckon you're right as rain about that. I tell you what, as soon as Jubal and I get something figured out, we'll have a meeting with all the hands and explain everything. How's that sound?"

"That'll do," Ned said, and he led the horses away.

"Men sound worried," I said.

"I would be too in their place, but it's not really their fight, unless they want it to be."

"I always thought when you ride for a brand, you accept all the troubles that come with it."

"That's not the way I see it. If a man wants to fight for the brand, I leave it up to him. He can always ride away. I'll give a high recommendation for another job, no hard feelings."

CHAPTER FIVE

We were almost to the house when I smelled an aroma coming out of the window. "My belly is talking to me. I'm needing nourishment."

The door opened and, there before my eyes, was the most beautiful sight I had ever seen. Even though it had only been a few hours, I was floored by her features.

"How'd it go?" Ruby asked.

"Not good," Bernie said.

"Does this mean there's going to be fighting?"

"More'n likely," Bernie said.

"Somebody could be killed. And for what? A piece of land?" Ruby was shouting.

"You don't understand, Ruby. It don't do nobody no good for you to get upset. We need to keep his cattle off our land if we're going to survive for another year. It's real simple."

"Why can't you survive together, the way you have been all these years?" she asked.

"Because he's greedy. He runs absolutely too many cattle on the land. If it was just his cows, then it might be enough, but when you add my horses, the grass isn't enough to feed them all."

Ruby said, "I'm going to check on supper." Then she turned and left the room.

"When were you planning on starting on this fence?" I asked.

"I was waiting for the dynamite. I've got the wire stashed in the barn. I reckon we can start anytime. What are your thoughts on it?" Bernie asked.

"I don't think we should start without posting guards with the fence builders," I said.

"I don't have enough hands for that."

"Then we should head into town and hire some more," I told him.

"Alright, first thing in the morning we'll go to town. I think I know who to see about some reliable men. Let's check if supper's ready, I'm getting mighty hungry."

Sandra had created another masterpiece. There was smothered steak, mashed potatoes and gravy, green beans, bread with butter, and a pie for dessert.

"Sandra, do you cook this way all the time?" I asked her.

"No, I cook only for Mr. Cantrell and myself. I cook a big meal because you and the young miss are here."

"Well, I want to say this is one of the best meals I have had in a very long time. Thank you for the extra effort you put into it."

"Thank you for saying that. I enjoy cooking much more when someone tells me they enjoy what I cook."

"Sandra has had offers from three of the large ranches to come and work for them, but she decided she wanted to be here. Ain't that so, Sandra?" Bernie asked.

I watched as Sandra looked at Bernie, and I knew why she wanted to stay with him. She was sweet on Bernie, and the old fool didn't even know it.

"We better hit the hay if we're leaving for town at first light," Bernie said.

"You gonna ride into town with us, Ruby?" I asked.

"Sure, I'd like to go, if that's alright with you, Uncle Bernie? I would like to check out the general store and get a few things."

"I reckon it's alright. You can do your shopping while we check on some men."

"Of course, but I don't have a horse," Ruby said.

"You want to ride in the wagon?" I asked.

"That thing was so darn rough and bumpy. I think I would rather ride in a saddle, that way the horse will feel all the bumps. You do have a horse for me, don't you, Uncle Bernie?"

"Do I have a horse for you? Did you forget this is a horse ranch? I have the perfect blue roan mare for you. She's real gentle and easy to handle, and she's smaller than most of the other horses. I'll show her to you right after breakfast tomorrow." Bernie started walking away.

"What about me? You want me to ride the same one I rode to Renfros?" I asked.

"No. I've got another one picked out for you, but you might not want it."

"Why's that?"

"I figure it's gonna pull up lame in a couple days. I sure wouldn't want you to have to go through that again."

"Bernie! I don't like to kid around about things like that," I said.

"It's good to see you two getting along so well," Ruby said smiling.

"Goodnight to you both," Bernie said and walked away.

Early the next morning, after one of Sandra's meals, Bernie said, "Let's get the animals and head into town. We're burning daylight."

We walked into the barn and the two men that were forking hay into the loft were just finishing up.

"Ned, go get the big black out of the small corral and bring him around. Drew, you go get the roan mare, saddle her, and bring her around," Bernie told them.

They both nodded affirmative and took off in different directions.

"I know both of you are gonna be pleased with the horses I picked for you," Bernie said with a bit of excitement.

Ned came in the back door, leading a big black stallion. The horse was beautiful. He looked as if he could run for a 100 miles and not be winded.

"Thanks, Ned. Jubal, this is your horse," Bernie said.

"He's a beauty, Bernie. Is he a thoroughbred?" I asked.

"That he is, and he belongs to you free and clear."

"Bernie, I can't accept this animal. He's worth too much," I argued.

"Jubal, I figure I owe you a horse for the one that went lame on you. You just take good care of him and I'll be pleased."

Just then, Drew came around the corner leading a small blue roan mare. She was tiny beside the stallion.

"Oh, she's beautiful," exclaimed Ruby. "I love her. Are you going to give her to me like you gave the black to Jubal?"

"Of course, of course. She belongs to you. You do know how to ride, don't you?" he teased.

"Oh, Uncle Bernie. Don't insult me, please?"

CHAPTER SIX

"Okay, let's go to town," he said to the two of us.

The road had mostly dried from the storm so it wasn't too hard on the horses, and we reached town a little before noon.

"Homer Reid, the newspaper editor, knows everything that happens in this town, and even outside of it," Bernie said. "If there are any cowboys needing work, he'll know."

"I'm going to the store to pick up a few things for the house. Where do you want to meet after I get through?" asked Ruby.

"I'd like for you to wait at the store until I come and pick you up," I told her. "A young lady shouldn't be wandering the streets alone."

"I do believe I'm old enough to take care of myself," Ruby huffed.

"I'll come pick you up in, say half an hour, then we'll go back to the newspaper office. It should be around dinner time, so we can go eat at Kreagan's Cafe."

"If you insist," she said. "I'll see you in half an hour, then."

We stopped in front of the general store where we left Ruby, then rode on to the newspaper office at the end of

Main Street. We dismounted and tied the reins to the hitching rail, then walked into the office.

Homer Reid was sitting at a big oak desk shuffling papers, and didn't see or hear us enter. We were almost to his desk before he looked up. "Well hello, Bernie. What brings you to town in the middle of the week?"

"Homer, this is Jubal Foxworth. He's helping me with a little problem out at the ranch."

"I know Mr. Foxworth by reputation. I believe Ned Buntline wrote some stories about you in some of those dime novels."

"I wouldn't believe everything you read. Being a newspaper man, you should know that."

He nodded and said, "You are right about that. What kind of trouble are you having, Bernie?"

"I've decided to fence my property, and Renfro is upset about it. He's not caused any trouble yet, but he made some pretty serious threats. Jubal suggested we hire some men to guard the workers as they build the fence. I was hoping you'd know of some honest, hard-working men."

"Just so happens Rafferty had to lay off half his hands. Those are some of the best workers around, and they're looking for work."

"Why'd Rafferty lay them off?"

"You haven't heard?" asked Homer. "He lost his wife a few days ago and decided it was time to think about retiring. You know he was one of the first settlers in the county. Anyway, if you want to hire them boys, you'll find them over at the Lucky Dog Saloon."

"Thanks, Homer. Be sure and tell the missus I said hello."

"I'll do that," said Homer. "I understand your niece is visiting with you?"

"She's not visiting, she's gonna be staying with me. She lost her parents in an accident a few months back, so I invited her to come."

"I'd like to meet her and introduce her to my missus when she comes to town."

"She's over at the general store right now. Tell you what, why not come with us to Kreagan's Café? We're gonna go there for dinner."

"I am getting a little hungry," Homer said. "You did say you were buying, didn't you?"

"Sure, I'll buy dinner for you."

Homer picked up a pad and stuck a pencil in his shirt pocket. "I'm ready. I always carry a pencil and paper with me. Can't never tell when I'll see or hear something worth putting in the paper."

We walked to the general store, and Ruby was standing at the counter conversing with Mrs. Milligan, the owner's wife.

We said hello to Mrs. Milligan, then asked Ruby if she was ready.

"Yes, I'm ready. Goodbye to you, Mrs. Milligan. If you'll send word to the ranch when those items come in, I would appreciate it."

"I'll do that, Miss Cantrell," said Mrs. Milligan. "Goodbye."

"Good day to you," we all said to her.

After walking the two blocks to the café, we went inside. As soon as we were settled, Bernie said, "Ruby, this is Homer Reid. He owns and operates the local newspaper."

"I'm glad to finally meet Bernie's niece. He's had nothing but good things to say about you," Reid said. "I'd like for you to stop by the office sometime, and I'll take you to meet my wife. I'm sure the two of you can find something to talk about."

"I'm pleased to meet someone who's a friend of Uncle Bernie. And I would love to meet your wife. Perhaps I can stop by before we leave town," Ruby said.

She looked at me and asked, "Did you find some men to hire?"

"I think so," I answered. "Mr. Reid told us about a couple who are looking for work. Soon as we're finished eating, we'll go and talk to them. Speaking of eating, here comes the waitress."

"Good day to you folks, what can I get for you today?"

"I want a big steak and all the fixings," Bernie said.

"That sounds like a good idea," I said.

"Can you cut one of those big steaks in half for me," asked Ruby.

"I'll have the other half," said Reid.

"I'll be right back with your drinks. Tea okay for everybody?"

"Tea will be fine," Reid answered as he looked us all. "And by the way, Mr. Foxworth, please call me Homer."

"I'll do that, if you'll call me Jubal."

"I just thought of something else you need to know," said Homer.

"What's that?" I asked.

"There's been a few hard cases ride into town the last couple of days. Since you told me about Renfro, I now know why."

"You figure he's hired some guns?" I asked.

"Only reason they would be coming in, best I can figure. Somebody said one of them is Rudolph Guntherson."

"I've heard of him," Bernie said. "You heard of him, Jubal?"

"Yeah, I heard about him."

"Ever tangle with him?" asked Bernie.

"If I had, one of us wouldn't be here now."

"I reckon that's so," said Bernie. "Hey, I just remembered, you're the deputy sheriff, ain't you?"

"The nighttime deputy."

"You need to check in with the sheriff while we're in town?" Bernie asked.

"Nope. He knew it was a temporary thing with me. But I've got a better question for you."

"What?"

"Have you checked in with the sheriff about your trouble?"

"Did the first time Renfro threatened me. Sheriff said until somebody did something more than threaten, he couldn't do nothing. I lost my temper and told him it would be too late after somebody did something. He apologized, and I left."

"The law is a funny business sometimes. I reckon we need to go see those men that need a job, don't you?" I asked Bernie.

"While you two are busy hiring someone, I think I'll go visit with Mrs. Reid, if Mr. Reid will take me," Ruby said.

"Sure, she will be so happy to have a visitor, and please call me Homer."

"Alright, we've got all that figured out. Homer, you take good care of Ruby. Ruby, we'll see you later," Bernie said. "Let's go, Jubal."

We left the cafe and walked to the saloon. The closer we got, the louder the noise got.

"Take the tie-down off your gun." I got mine ready, too.

"You expecting trouble?" he asked.

"Can't never tell. Always be ready. I'll go in first." I pushed through the doors, stepping to the side while my eyes adjusted to the dimly-lit room. Bernie came in and settled on the other side. I scanned the busy room that was crowded with people, and didn't see an empty table anywhere. The bar was so packed men were standing double, having to reach over one another to get a drink.

"It's gonna be hard to locate them," Bernie said.

"Let's see the bartender." I started making my way to the bar. "Maybe he can point them out to us."

"Gonna be hard to get to him through that crowd," Bernie said.

I walked to the first table and said, "Excuse me? Would you mind standing up?"

"What for?" he asked.

"Just humor me, please?"

He stood, and I stepped onto the chair and up onto the table and yelled, "Hey! Listen up!"

Nothing. No one heard me.

"Mister, you need to get down off our table," the man standing beside the chair said.

"This is really important." I looked down at him. "Bear with me for a minute. Please?"

"If it's important, we'll help you." He beckoned for his friends to stand also. "Start hollering!"

We all started yelling as loud as we could, then the piano stopped, the people stopped talking, and it got very quiet.

Soon, voices starting speaking from the place. "What is it? What's going on?"

"Look at that cowboy standing on the table."

"Ain't he the deputy sheriff?"

"Yeah, but he only deputies at night."

"Wonder what he wants?"

"Listen, he's saying something."

"Speak up, we can't hear you!"

"I'm in here looking for the men who worked for Rafferty," I said.

"That must be us." Four cowboys stood.

"What do you want with us? We ain't done nothing," one of them said.

"Let's step outside away from this crowd and I'll fill you in." I jumped to the floor. "Here you go." I shoved a couple dollars to the men who helped me. "Buy yourselves a drink."

They thanked me and I walked outside, where Bernie was already in a conversation with the four men.

"You telling me there might be gunplay?" the tall, thin man asked.

"There could be. In fact, there more than likely will be," Bernie replied.

"Rowdy, we ain't got nobody else offering to take us on," said a young man.

"Yeah," another man spoke up. "We need to find work or head south where we might, and I stress might, sign on a trail herd."

"We'd expect more than regular wages, since we might have to use our guns. You realize we're not gunmen, we're just regular, everyday cow punchers," the one called Rowdy said.

"I understand that. Wouldn't expect you to work for regular wages," said Bernie. "And to top it off, if there is gunplay, there'll be a bonus. How's that sound?"

Rowdy looked at the other three men. They shook their heads affirmatively.

"Alright, Mr. Cantrell, you got yourselves some guards for your fence builders. When you want us to start?"

"You can come on back with us if you want. We'll leave as soon as we pick up my niece. Should be ready in, say, half an hour. Meet us at the livery stable."

"We'll be there," Rowdy said.

Bernie and I walked away and headed to the edge of town where Homer Reid's house was located. It was a pretty little white house with blue shutters.

'Sure would be nice to settle down in a place like this with the right woman. Now what brought up that thought? Is Ruby affecting me that much?'

"Here we are. Hold up! Where you going? You were going to walk past the place," Bernie said.

"I was just thinking about something."

"I guess you were. Care to share with me what had you so tangled up?"

"Just some personal stuff. Sure is a pretty little place, ain't it?"

"I guess newspaper business does fairly well," he said. "Here comes Ruby now."

Homer, his wife Nelda, and Ruby came out the door and met us at the gate.

"I spotted you through the window and thought you'd want to head back to the ranch as soon as you could," Ruby said.

"Did you hire the men?" Homer asked.

"Yes, we hired four of Rafferty's men," Bernie answered. "They seem like good men. The older one, Rowdy, worked for Rafferty for almost five years. Man don't last that long if he's not reliable."

"Well, thanks for steering us to them. I'm beholden to you." Bernie turned, looking like he was ready to head out. "I reckon we better start back if we want to beat the darkness. So long."

"I've really enjoyed visiting with you, Nelda," Ruby said. "Maybe you can come see me at the ranch some time."

"I'll try, if I can get Homer away from his newspaper long enough to drive me." She smiled.

"You get him to bring you out. I'll teach you to drive a wagon or ride a horse, whichever you want. How's that sound to you?"

"I'm glad I finally got to meet you, Jubal." Homer reached out his hand to shake. "Thanks for setting me straight about Buntline's writing."

"My pleasure, Homer, come say howdy when you bring your wife out."

Ruby, Bernie, and I walked back to the horses, then we led them down the street to the livery stable. The four newly-hired men were waiting.

"You boys ready to travel?" asked Bernie.

"We're ready, Boss. Lead the way." Rowdy waved for the others to follow.

We all mounted our animals and headed out of town. We had just reached the end of Main Street when Homer came running up behind us hollering, "Hold up, wait!"

We pulled up and turned the animals toward him.

"What's the matter?" Bernie asked.

"The sheriff's been killed. That Guntherson fellow did it. He was stirring up trouble in the saloon and, when the sheriff came in, he didn't even wait for him to say anything, just shot him down in cold blood. Then he looked at the people still in the saloon and said, 'Y'all saw it. It was self-defense. Now one of you go find a man called Foxworth and tell him I'll be waiting right here. And while you're at it, get this carcass out of here.'"

"Two men picked up the sheriff's body and carried it out," Homer said. "That's when someone came to me, knowing you had been in town to see me."

"I reckon I better go see this fellow," I said.

"Oh, Jubal," exclaimed Ruby. "Isn't there another way?"

"If I don't finish it now, it'll come up again. You can't run from it."

"Promise me you'll be careful," she pleaded.

"Always. Even more so now that I've got somebody to come back to."

"We're not gunslingers, but we're willing to back your play," Rowdy said.

"I appreciate that, but this is a two-man party, and you boys aren't invited."

"Good luck, Jubal," Bernie said. "We'll be waiting at the stable."

"Take my horse with you. I'll walk from here," I told him.

CHAPTER SEVEN

A walk like this can seem like an eternity, even though it's only a few yards. I thought this kind of thing wasn't gonna happen anymore, but I guess I was mistaken. I stopped in front of the saloon and hollered for Guntherson to come out.

What seemed like minutes passed, though it was probably just seconds, and he came through the swinging doors.

He was a big, ugly man, dressed in dusty, well-worn black clothes, but his black leather holster and Pearl-handled .45 looked brand new. A really dedicated gunman always takes very good care of his weapon, since his life depends on it.

"I understand you were inquiring about me," I said.

"Your name Foxworth?" he snarled.

"It is."

"They tell me you used to be fast; faster than a rattlesnake, and twice as deadly."

"Yeah, I heard that too." I was still unconcerned.

"I'm from Missouri. Folks from there have to see something for themselves before they believe it. You want to show me?"

"Not particularly."

"What's the matter? You turn yellow in your old age?"

"Not at all. Just gotten a little smarter. I finally realized there's no purpose to that sort of thing."

"I think you're yellow." He was still taunting me.

"I really don't care what you think or do, but I would appreciate you doing something besides shooting your mouth off."

He was fast, very fast, but I was a tad faster. He was lying in the street on his back, staring up at nothing. His hand was gripping his bright, shiny .45, and his thumb was still on the hammer.

A crowd suddenly appeared. "You're Jubal Foxworth, ain't you?" someone asked.

I ignored the questions being thrown at me, and walked away from the dead man lying in the street.

When I reached the livery stable, Ruby came rushing out the door and flung herself into my arms. "Oh, Jubal. I was so afraid I'd never see you again."

"I'm here, and I'm okay. Let's go home." Home. That sure did have a nice ring to it. "I ain't never had a place I could call home."

"You've got one now, and there's a pretty girl that goes with it," Ruby said, then winked at me.

She slipped her arm in mine and we walked to where Bernie and the boys were waiting.

"I see you made it through that little trouble okay," Bernie said.

"I'm here, ain't I?"

Rowdy walked over to us. "I heard that fellow Guntherson was faster than greased lightning."

"He was."

"How'd you beat him if he was so fast?" the youngest cowboy asked.

"Kid, if you have to ask that, you wouldn't understand the answer. The only thing you need to know is don't become a gunfighter, 'cause someday it might be you lying in the street staring at nothing,"

"Let's head home. I think we've all had enough excitement for a while," Bernie said.

We got back to the ranch late in the day. The yellow glow from the setting sun was sneaking its light through the tree branches and causing odd-shaped shadows to fall all around.

"Isn't that a beautiful sight," Ruby asked. "I love this time of day."

"You boys follow me." Bernie waved his arm as he headed back. "I'll show you where you're gonna bunk."

The four men fell in behind Bernie, and they started riding toward the bunkhouse.

"We may as well take our horses to the barn," Ruby said to me.

"Might as well."

We reached the barn door and dismounted, then I took the reins of her horse and led both inside.

Ruby followed behind. "You didn't say anything when I commented on the beautiful sunset."

"It is a pretty sight, but my eyes were busy admiring something more beautiful."

"Oh, what's that?

"I think you are the most beautiful woman I have ever laid eyes on. And I want very much to kiss you."

"Now? Right here? Now?" She pretended to be nervous.

"Come here." I grabbed her, pulled her against me, and kissed her with all the pent-up passion in me.

She kissed me back with what I felt matched my passion. We stood there like that for what seemed like an eternity, but was in reality only a few seconds.

"We need to go inside," she said." It will be bedtime before long."

"I hope we have supper first. Sandra is one of the best cooks I've ever met."

"Yes, she does a good job, but I wonder . . . "

"What do you wonder?" I asked.

"I wonder if she can cook guinea eggs?" She gave me a sweet side grin.

"Not as good as someone I know." I had to tease her back.

"Come on." She looped her arm in mine and we went into the house.

We had just closed the door when Bernie opened it and came in. "Well, they're settled in. I introduced them to Ned and told'em we'd have a meeting first thing in the morning to explain what we're going to do. Now let's see if supper is ready?"

We gathered around the table waiting for Sandra to serve the meal.

"Shouldn't someone tell her we're here?" Ruby asked.

"Believe me, she knows everything that happens in this house," Bernie said as he sat down. "She'll be here any minute now."

Sure enough, she came through the door carrying two large platters, one with a roast smothered in onions, and the other with a bowl of mashed potatoes.

"It looks and smells delicious, as always," I said.

She didn't act as though she heard me. "I'll go get the rest of it, although it may be a little cool."

"She don't like it when I'm late without letting her know," Bernie said.

"If I were you, I'd do my best to make that woman happy," I told him.

"She's very well compensated for what she does here. I don't know any other way to make her happy."

"How long has she been with you?" Ruby asked.

"Let's see, I reckon . . . "

"It's been almost ten years," Sandra said. "And in all those years, I've not heard even one thank you from you, Bernie Cantrell."

"Sandra, don't you know how much I appreciate you?"

"Knowing it and hearing it is two separate things," she said and left the room.

"You know what I think, Bernie?" I asked him.

"What?"

"I do believe Sandra is sweet on you."

"I think so too," Ruby said.

"Surely not." Bernie looked at us like we were crazy. "Why she's been cooking and taking care of the house since even before Mildred died. She can't feel that way about me."

"Maybe you need to take a second look," I said. "Right now, let's partake of this wonderful meal that she has prepared."

Bernie filled his plate and set it down, then pushed his chair back and stood up.

"What's the matter, Uncle Bernie?" Ruby looked concerned.

"I need to talk to Sandra."

"Can't it wait until you eat?" Ruby asked.

"No, it can't wait." He rushed out.

"I do believe Uncle Bernie's eyes have been opened," Ruby said.

"That's what happens when love comes into the picture," I said. "You begin to see things more clearly than ever before."

"Are you seeing things more clearly, Jubal?" she asked.

"Absolutely. I've always been sort of confused about what I wanted out of life, but right now, right at this moment, I'm looking at what I want."

"And I'm looking at what I want," she said.

"You're wonderful." I leaned in close and wiped a dab of gravy off her chin, then stuck it in my mouth and winked.

She winked back, and we finished the meal conversing quietly about the things we wanted to share with one another. It's kind of funny how you search your whole life for the perfect mate, and then out of the blue she walks in and you know she's the one.

CHAPTER EIGHT

There was a loud banging on the door.

"Maybe we should see who it is," Ruby said. "It must be important or they wouldn't be banging so loud."

Bernie opened the door to Cletus Murphy, the sheriff's helper.

"Hello, Bernie, is Foxworth here?" He spotted me and pushed by Bernie. "The sheriff's asking for you, Foxworth."

"They said he was dead," I said, surprised. "He's okay, then?"

"Doctor says he ain't got much longer, but he's calling for you. Can you come?"

"Of course, I'll be back as soon as I can," I told Ruby.

"Please be careful," she said.

Bernie looked at me. "You want me to go with you?"

"No, you need to get things organized around here. We need to get started on that fence or we ain't never gonna get it done."

Murphy was already out the door. "I got an extra horse so's you don't have to saddle yours." He handed me the reins.

We mounted and took off toward town, without any conversation, because we were pushing the animals pretty hard. We rode straight to the doctor's office and dismounted.

Murphy took the reins of my horse. "I'll cool'em off, and then I'll be in. You go on in and see Neville."

"Thanks," I told him, and went inside.

"There you are, Foxworth, and none too soon. He's been asking for you since he regained consciousness. He's in here." Murphy motioned toward the open door.

I walked inside and saw that big, burly man lying in bed looking so very weak.

The sheriff was a tall and lean man, who sported a thick salt and pepper mustache. He'd always looked as though he could handle any trouble that arose, but lying in that death bed, I hardly recognized him. His once sun-browned skin was an almost ghostly white, his breathing was labored, and he looked extremely weak. He saw me, and I thought I saw a little flicker of a smile cross his face, but it disappeared just as quickly.

"Hello, Neville. You don't look any worse for wear. How come you asked me to come? It sounded urgent."

"Be serious. I ain't got time to kid around,"

"What is it you need, friend?"

He reached and grabbed my hand. "I need you to take over the sheriff job. There ain't nobody else qualified. You're the only one."

"We done talked about this a hundred times, Neville."

"Please don't fuss with a dying man, Jube? Please?"

The doctor came in the room. "You need to rest now, Neville."

"I'll be getting plenty of rest in a bit. Just let me and Jubal settle this first."

"Alright." The doctor gave up for the moment and left the room.

"What's it gonna be, Jubal Foxworth?" he asked, almost out of breath.

"I reckon you ain't giving me much choice, are you? Now why don't you rest and get better?"

"You know that ain't gonna happen, and I need to tell you what to expect as the new sheriff."

"I reckon I know enough without you exerting yourself."

"Guntherson didn't shoot me. Doc said I was shot in the back. Guntherson's bullet musta went wild. I know he didn't come to town alone. There's flyer's on all but one of them." He started coughing and spitting blood.

"Okay, he's got to stop talking now," the doctor said as he came back in the room.

"Just a couple more things, doc." He looked up at me. "Jube, the flyers are on my desk. The young guy don't have a flyer on him, but somebody said he was Guntherson's little brother. He's the one you need to watch for. I think he was the one who shot me. Now you take my badge, it's lying on the dresser there. Just pin it on and you'll be sheriff."

I walked over to the dresser, picked up the badge, and pinned it on.

"One last thing," Neville said.

"What's that?"

"Be careful, and good luck. See you when you get there." He closed his eyes.

The doctor stepped to his side and felt for a pulse, but Sheriff Neville Rynhard was gone—shot in the back by an unknown assailant. It was my job as sheriff to find his killer.

Dr. Aiken pulled the blanket up over his face.

"How many people know he was shot in the back?" I asked.

"No one, I guess. Why?"

"Let's keep it that way until I can figure out who did it?"

"Sure, I can do that. The undertaker will find out when he buries the body, but I suppose he could be persuaded to not tell anyone."

"Thanks, doc. I'll see you a little later." I left and went to the sheriff's office. Cletus was there.

"Murphy, I need you to do something for me."

"Yes sir, Sheriff. He's gone, ain't he?" He looked at the badge I was wearing. "Whatever you need, just ask."

"Yes, he's gone. He was a good man, and it's a shame that he had to die. Now I need you to ride out to Cantrell's ranch and tell them I'll be staying in town for a while."

"I'm on my way."

"Murphy?"

"Yeah?"

"What exactly did you do for the sheriff?"

"Most anything he didn't want to do hisself. I don't reckon you knew he helped a lot of folks down on their luck. Like you said, he was a good man. A real good man, I better git going." He turned and left the office in a somber mood.

I sat down at the desk and started looking through the flyers. I recognized a lot of the names, though I thought the majority of them would be dead by now. If Renfro was hiring these men, then our work was cut out for us. Bernie's hands weren't professional gunman like this bunch. We were greatly outnumbered.

I picked up the first five posters, folded them, and put them in my pocket. I got up and walked across the street, pausing at the door of the saloon. I was tall enough to look over the doors, so I could see the room was almost full.

I pushed through, stopping long enough for my eyes to adjust to the semi darkness. I then stepped to the end of the bar closest to the door. "Anybody in here named Guntherson?"

"Who's asking?" asked a pink-faced youngster. He was wearing two new Colt .45s low on his hips.

"You take a closer look, and you'll see the sheriff is asking."

"Sheriff's dead." He stood up straight as if he thought it would make him scarier. "I think maybe you as the new sheriff should turn and walk out the way you came in."

I looked up from under the brim of my hat and saw one of the men standing beside him mumbling something to him.

"What was it you said?" I asked him.

He began to look worried, unsure what I would do if I heard him correctly.

I asked him again. "What did you say?"

"I didn't say nothing."

"Really? I'm sure I heard you say that I should move along. Isn't that what you said?"

"That was a mistake," he said with a shaky voice. "I didn't know who you was until somebody told me."

"Now why would that make a difference to a big, brave gunman like yourself?"

"I heard about you. You're Jubal Foxworth. You're the one shot Rudy. They say you're faster than a mad rattle snake, and twice as deadly. I don't want to be your next victim."

"You don't have to be a victim. I always give a man a choice. You can turn and head over to the jail if that's what you want."

"You gonna shoot me in the back?" he asked.

"I ain't never done that, and I don't intend to start now. If you want to go to jail, then lay your guns on the bar and go."

The young man started pulling his pistols out of the holsters.

"I'd do that really slow and carefully if I was you."

He laid the pistols on the bar one at a time, then turned and walked through the swinging doors.

I started in behind him, and heard a conversation between a couple men.

"Did you see that? He faced that kid down without drawing his weapon."

"Do you know who he is?"

"Don't know him. I didn't know anybody could be so fast."

"How do you know he's fast? He didn't draw."

"That young gunman seemed to know who he is."

"Why don't you ask him?"

"Not me. Why don't you?"

The kid and I reached the jail. "Go ahead inside," I told him.

"If I can ask, why you locking me up? I didn't do nothing."

"I believe you'll come up with a lot of reasons, if you'll think on it. The main reason, however, is I believe you shot the sheriff in the back."

"Everyone saw Rudy shoot him. And it wasn't in the back," he argued.

"Did you see it?" I asked.

"Well, uh, no." He hesitated. "I wasn't there."

"Where were you?"

"I . . . uh . . . I was busy someplace else."

"You were across the street from the saloon and, when the sheriff got there, you shot him in the back. I've got witnesses that saw you."

"There wasn't anybody on the street, I looked."

"You may as well admit it, kid. This is one that your big brother can't help you get out of."

"He told me to do it. I didn't want to do it, but he made me."

"That ain't gonna make no difference to the jury. "Come on back and pick a cell."

"Please, mister Foxworth, I don't want to hang. Rudy made me do it."

"How old are you, kid?"

"I'll be eighteen in a few days."

"That's plenty old enough to make your own decisions. And to pay for them when you make a wrong one. You know any of the fellows that Renfro hired?"

"I don't know nobody named Renfro," he said.

"Alright. You rest easy, I'll be back."

CHAPTER NINE

I had just stepped off the wooden sidewalk and glanced up at the roof across the street when a slug hit the hitching rail next to my hand. I fell and rolled to the left, landing behind a barrel that was sitting at the corner of the building. I raised up enough to take a gander at the rooftop where the shot came from. I didn't see anyone, so I stood slowly. Nothing. No shots. The shooter must have gone. I stepped from behind the barrel and scanned the rooftops and street.

It was extremely quiet for this time of day. It always amazed me the way folks hid when there was trouble brewing. Of course I couldn't blame them, I wouldn't want to get in the middle of people shooting at one another.

I stepped back up on the sidewalk and started walking down the street, always vigilant as to the movements around me. I saw a few of the business owners pull their shades down as I walked past. I kept walking until I reached the end of Main Street.

I stood there, undecided about which way to go. There were two more saloons in town, one in each direction on Second Street.

Might as well try the Two Door saloon, since it was closer. I returned my six gun to the holster and stayed on the sidewalk where it was less likely someone could hit me from the same side without showing himself.

When I got closer to the saloon, I noticed it was quiet—too quiet for a saloon, even this time of day. There were three horses tied at the hitching rail, and they were lathered, as if they had been ridden hard.

I reached the swinging doors and stopped. Something didn't feel right. I placed my back against the wall next to the right side of the door. "You fellows inside there need to come on out so's we can get better acquainted," I said loudly.

The doors slammed back from the impact of the bullets hitting them, so I slid a little further away from them. There was a window on the other side of the doors from where I was. *Too risky.*

I kept sliding against the wall until I reached the corner, then I dropped off the sidewalk and walked down the alley to the back of the saloon. I tried the back door. It wasn't locked, so I opened it cautiously and went inside. I sneaked to the door separating the back room from the main one and listened.

"What's he waiting for? Why don't he come on in?"

"From what I heard about him, he don't take no chances. But he will be coming in, you can count on it."

"I wish he would hurry; I need a drink."

I pushed the door open, with my pistol cocked and ready. "You boys waiting for me. I've got you covered."

The one closest to me turned and threw a shot in my direction. He missed by a mile since he was in a hurry.

I let loose with a shot that knocked him back into the table he was standing beside and his body sprawled across the top, scattering glasses and bottles in all directions.

The other two took cover, one behind the bar, the other turning a table over before hiding behind it.

I, in the meantime, had overturned a table beside the door and knelt down behind it. "You boys need to give up if you expect to walk out of here alive tonight."

Their answer was three shots thudding into the table top. I slid my gun around the edge of the table and let loose with two shots. I didn't expect to hit anything, just let them know that I was still here.

"You boys working for Renfro?" I asked. "Or are you here with Guntherson?"

"Renfro said you would be an easy target. I'm beginning to think he wasn't being truthful," said the one behind the bar.

"Like I said, if you want to live, give up."

"How about you just let us walk out of here?" he asked. "And not come back?"

"That might have worked if the sheriff hadn't been killed when you boys came into town."

"We didn't have nothing to do with that. That was Guntherson trying to prove to everybody how tough he was. We wasn't part of the sheriff getting killed."

"Give up and tell that to a jury. Maybe they'll believe you."

"Do you believe us?" he sounded desperate.

"It don't matter what I believe. It's the judge and jury you got to convince. Now, what's it going to be? Jail or the undertaker?"

"Okay, I'm coming out. You coming out, Jory?"

"I'm coming out."

"Let me see both your guns slide across the floor, and come on out with your hands in the air," I told them.

A .45 slid across the floor, followed by another a little later.

"Alright boys. Come on out. Remember, I've got you covered."

They were both young, probably in their twenties, and dressed like normal drovers. They stood there with their hands in the air, looking like the cat that just ate the canary.

"What made you boys take this job?" I asked. "You don't look like gunmen."

"It sounded like easy money. All we had to do was scare you from building a fence," said the tall one. "Nobody said nothing about having to face Jubal Foxworth."

"You live and learn, and this time I hope you learned to check into it before you accept a job. There ain't no such thing as easy money. Come on." I bent down and picked up their guns. "The jail's this way."

"What about Reggie? We just gonna leave him lying there?" he asked.

"The undertaker'll be along in a while. He'll take good care of him. Was he a close friend?"

"He was. A real close friend. He tried to talk us out of taking this job," he said. "Should've listened to him."

"The sheriff was a real good friend of mine," I said.

"Listen. I swear we didn't have nothing to do with that."

"Let's go." I nodded toward the door.

I followed the two cowboys out, and we walked down the sidewalk and into the jail.

"Guntherson?" I asked. "You know these men?"

"I seen'em in the saloon, but no, I don't know them. Why?"

"They didn't ride in with you and your brother?"

"Naw. Abner, Earl, Wyatt, me, and Rudy came in together. These fellows are strangers to me." He didn't realize he had just given me the names of the men I was looking for.

"I tell you boys what. I'm gonna let you go, on one condition."

"Sure. Anything. Anything at all," the tall one said.

"You climb on your horses and don't hesitate any as you leave town. Don't even think about looking back, or it'll be worse for you than it was for Lot's wife when she looked."

"We sure do appreciate this, Mister Foxworth. Can we have our guns back?"

I handed them their weapons. They slid them into the holsters, nodded to me, and left the room. I watched as they patted each other on the back and jumped in the air. Just two youngsters looking to make some easy money.

"You let them fellows go. Why can't you do the same for me?" Guntherson whined.

"They didn't shoot nobody in the back. You did. However, you can do something that might keep you from hanging."

"What? I'd do most anything to keep the noose from around my neck."

"Tell me where I can find the men that rode into town with you."

"When they're in town, they hang out at the Howling Hound saloon. Harry is sweet on one of the girls there. Does that help you?"

"Maybe, we'll see." I left the jail and stopped in the local eating establishment to have a bowl of chili with a lot of onions and crackers. I liked lots of onions in my chili. I paid for the meal and walked south on Main Street, then crossed over to the end of Second Street. The Howling Hound saloon had the right name—at least tonight it did.

What made this saloon so different from the others was as I got closer, I could hear singing, and not very bad either. Of course I couldn't make out all the words because of the roar of the men.

Just then, I heard a man's voice yelling for everybody to shut up. The noise stopped, and I heard another voice ask what he thought he was doing.

"I didn't mean nothing, mister. I was just asking. You don't have to point your gun at me. Go ahead and say your peace."

"I'm only gonna tell you this one time, so you better listen real good. When the lady is singing, I don't want to hear anything but her voice. Does everybody understand?"

As I watched from the door, no one said anything. Probably because he was waving his pistol around.

I stood at the entrance, peering over the door. The place was crowded, but there was an empty circle in the center where the man was standing with his pistol in his hand. He was the one doing all the hollering. I stood there watching until he put his gun back in the holster, then I pushed open the doors and stepped inside.

The man closest to the door took one look at me and moved aside, motioning the man next to him to move also. It continued that way until I was standing in front of the man in the center.

He looked me up and down. "Who are you, and what do you want? Can't you see the lady is singing here? We don't like interruptions."

"As for who I am, this badge should answer that question. As for as what I want? Well, I believe I want you and your friends to come to jail with me."

"What're you talking about? I ain't broke no laws that I know about," he slurred. "So you got no reason for bothering me or my friends."

"Maybe you ain't broke no laws yet, but I think you've got some ideas about breaking some in the near future."

"You can't arrest a man for what he's thinking."

"You'd be surprised at what I can or can't do. Now, you can either come peaceably, or we can do it the hard way."

I was gradually moving closer to him as we were talking. When I saw his hand move toward his weapon, I drew my .45 and laid the barrel next to his left ear.

He folded like an accordion.

"You didn't have no call to do that," one of his companions said.

"You want to join him?"

"No, I don't, but you can bet his buddies will be coming for him. You're just lucky they're not here now."

Tell them I'll be at the jail ready to take any and all complaints. Now a couple of you men carry this carcass over to the jail."

Three men hurried over, picked him up, and hustled him out the door.

"Sorry for breaking into your fun, but the law has a job to do."

I followed the men back to the jail, then rushed in front of them and opened the door.

"Hey, what's wrong with Harry?" Guntherson asked.

"He bumped his head on something," I told him. "You boys put him in the cell next to the kid, so's he won't feel lonesome when he wakes up."

"Why's everybody always calling me kid?" I don't like it."

Harry was already beginning to stir. He was groaning and rubbing his head. "Where am I? Hey, what am I doing in jail?"

"Hello, Harry," said the kid. "He got me, too. Did the boys get away?"

"Kid, you got a big mouth," Harry said.

"He knows all about everything," Guntherson said. "He knows we're working for Renfro and everything."

"It's a good thing Rudy ain't here, or you'd be in big trouble," Harry told the kid.

"You don't know, do you?" the kid asked Harry.

"Know what?"

"Rudy's dead. The new sheriff shot him."

"That right, Sheriff?" asked Harry. "You kill Rudolph Guntherson?"

"He didn't give me a choice."

"You must be fast," he said shaking his head.

"Fast enough," I replied. "Fast enough. You know what your other pards are up to?"

"I would guess they're where I should have been—out at Renfro's getting ready for a fight."

I left the jail and went to the livery stable to get my horse.

"You sure are locking a lot of folks up, ain't you?" asked Thad. Thaddeus T. Wingate was a scruffy-looking, small man, who was wearing dirty clothes. He was also the owner of the livery stable. "Where you going now?"

"Why don't you just get my horse for me," I told him. "The less you know about things the better."

"Alright, alright," he mumbled. "I's just asking." He left and returned with the horse Cletus had brought for me to tide. "If I might ask, where's that big Black you rode in here earlier? He's probably one of the best horses I've had in here in quite a while. He's sure a beauty."

"Thad, you finally said something that I'm glad to hear. I had to leave him at the ranch because I was in a hurry. I'll be back a little later."

CHAPTER TEN

It was right after sunup that I rode out to a little knoll looking down on Renfro's spread. I removed a spyglass that I had taken off a sailor in Cayuca County. It was just the thing I needed to watch Renfro's men without them seeing me.

The sailor was drunk, and thought he was a hot shot gunman. I hated to take his life, but when he drew and shot at me, missing with his first shot, I couldn't take a chance on him missing a second time. So I drew my weapon and told him to stop. When he pointed his pistol at me a second time, I pulled the trigger, causing his bullet to barely miss my head.

The witnesses told the sheriff it was self-defense and he ruled it justifiable, but said he would appreciate it if I would find someplace else to conduct my business. He handed me the sailor's belongings, and called them the spoils of war. The spyglass was part of those belongings. To the victor goes the spoils.

There were six men at Renfro's, and it looked as though they were getting ready to move out. I didn't understand why they were taking a wagon, unless they were planning on trying to take the wire. I turned away and started back to my horse, but stopped and turned back and put the glass to my eye.

I thought I recognized him. Ace Decker was his name, and that name stirred my memory. I knew I had heard it somewhere, but couldn't place when or where. I knew it would come to me sooner or later, but right now I had to go tell Bernie what I had seen.

I put the glass back in my saddlebags and mounted up. Surely, they wouldn't try anything before dark, but I needed to tell Bernie about this new situation. We needed to be ready for them if they did show up, so I took one last glance at the men and mounted up.

I began missing Ruby the moment I was out of sight. *What is it about love that takes control of a man's mind and body? Ruby Cantrell is indeed a very special person, and she has her hook in me.*

CHAPTER ELEVEN

I rode into the yard at Cantrell's Ranch and dismounted, then stood for a minute looking around. If Renfro's men were going to try anything, it probably wouldn't be until everybody was in bed.

Ned came out of the barn and walked over to me. "Want me to take your horse to the barn, Mr. Foxworth?"

"Sure, I appreciate that. You need to tell the boys to be alert. I think Renfro's boys are gonna try something tonight."

"Got any idea what?"

"Wish I did. They are bringing a wagon."

"That means they're gonna try to get the wire. I don't think they know about the dynamite . . . yet."

"Just tell all the men to be alert." I turned and walked to the house.

I was almost to the door when it opened and Ruby was standing there in the opening. She looked angelic with the light from the hallway behind her.

"Oh, Jubal. I'm so glad you're home. I missed you so very much."

I just stood where I was drinking in the beautiful sight in front of me.

"Well, are you just going to stand there?" she asked.

"I'm enjoying the view." I walked toward her, taking her in my arms when I reached her. She felt so right in my arms.

"Where have you been all my life?" I asked her.

"Waiting for you." She pulled my head down, and our lips met softly. Then, as we lingered, our breathing became labored.

I finally released her and stepped back. "Lordy, I missed you. I love you so much. I've never said that to a woman before."

"I love you very much, and I've never told a man that before," she said.

"Is that you, Jubal?" Bernie hollered. "What are you doing standing out there? Come on in. Tell me what you been doing."

Ruby stepped to the side so I could go in. She grabbed my arm as I passed and slipped hers inside mine.

"Come on in the parlor. We'll have a drink while you tell me everything," Bernie said. "You can come too, Ruby, unless you got something else to do."

"It's a little early for me," I said to Bernie.

"Maybe I'll check on breakfast. It's getting close." Ruby winked at me and left.

"You don't want a whiskey?" Bernie asked.

"I don't think so, I'll wait on breakfast. Whiskey might dull the taste of Sandra's cooking. By the way, you need to tell me what happened between you and Sandra."

"I'll tell you that after you fill me in on what you've been doing."

"Well, first of all, the sheriff didn't make it. He was shot in the back by Guntherson's kid brother. He didn't have a chance."

"You mean it wasn't Guntherson that shot him?"

"It seems Guntherson had lost some of his accuracy, so he had his brother shoot him as he walked through the saloon door. That way it looked like Guntherson shot him, when in reality his brother did."

"That's a damn shame," he said. "Neville was a good man. Then what happened? I suppose you killed the brother?"

"No, but I do have him and another gang member locked up."

"You have been busy," Bernie said. "I got the men started on it first thing this morning. You think Renfro's gonna try to stop us?"

"Yes, I stopped by his place up on that little hill where I could check them out, and I saw six men hooking up a wagon. I figure they're gonna try to steal the wire sometime tonight."

"I better tell the men," he said.

"I told Ned to tell them to be watching tonight. I hope it was alright for me to do that."

"Of course, you're in this with us," Bernie said.

"I've got it," I said loudly.

"Got what?" asked Bernie.

"I remember where I saw him,"

"Saw who? What are you talking about?"

"Ace Decker. I saw him with the rest of Renfro's men."

"So? What about him?" Bernie asked.

"He's a fast gun out of Ft. Bentley. He probably rode in with Guntherson. They used to travel together years ago, always arguing about which one of them was faster. They never did tangle with one another. They always picked out some poor pilgrim and used him to see who was faster."

"Sounds like a hard case," Bernie said.

"I hope I don't have to face him. Although I will if it comes down to it."

"Let's go on into the dining room and see if we can hurry Sandra up with breakfast."

"You gonna tell me what happened between the two of you?"

"Let's go on in and we'll both tell you," he answered.

Sandra and Ruby were just finishing setting the table.

"You boys finished just in time. Have a seat and we'll bring in the food," Ruby said.

"Before we sit, Sandra and I have an announcement," an excited Bernie announced. "We're gonna get married."

"Oh!" Ruby got all excited. "I'm so glad to hear that. I knew you cared for him."

"When is this event supposed to take place?" I asked.

"We thought we'd wait until the fence is built and this trouble is settled." He put his arm around Sandra.

"What have you got to say about all this, Sandra," I asked.

"I have been waiting for so long I had given up hope that it would ever happen. I'm just so, so happy."

"Now that Sandra is going to be Mrs. Cantrell, she should sit and eat with us," Ruby got up and pulled out a chair for Sandra.

"That's a splendid idea," Bernie said.

"But who will serve the meal?" Sandra hesitated to sit, obviously still feeling like it was her job.

"I think we should all pitch in," Bernie said.

"The rest of the dishes are in the kitchen," she said. "Should I go and get them, or are we all going?"

I headed for the kitchen with Ruby and Sandra on my heels, but Bernie was taking a little longer.

"This will take some getting used to," he said as he came up behind us. We all grabbed a dish of food and carried it back to the table.

It was a very enjoyable meal and fellowship. Sandra and Ruby were carrying on a very lively conversation.

When we were finished eating, Bernie said, "We probably should check on the men."

"That's a great idea. Right after we help clean up this mess," I told him.

"You men go ahead, Ruby can help me with cleaning up," Sandra said.

"Alright," Bernie conceded. "You talked me into it. Come on, Jube, let's check the weapons and ammunition. We sure don't want any hiccups in this operation."

"That sounds like a good idea. Goodbye, ladies," I said.

"See you girls later." Bernie turned and started to head out.

Both Ruby and Sandra said goodbye, then Bernie and I went into the parlor where he kept his rifles. We took them out and checked to make sure they were working well.

"Let's go check on the dynamite. Make sure it's covered real good," Bernie said.

We left the house and went to the barn.

"That's a lot of wire," I said.

"Gonna need every bit of it. Probably even more." Bernie grabbed a tarp and started to spread it out. "Here, help me tie this down on top."

"What are we gonna do if they discover the dynamite?" I asked.

"I hope we catch them before they do." Bernie pulled the tarp as far as it would go. "It only covers up half the wire, see?"

"Yeah, unless they start loading from the back side."

"Let's take a ride out and see how the boys are doing on the fence."

"Lead the way," I said. "I want to thank you again for the black. He's a fine animal."

"I'm glad you like him. It was worth the price of two or three horses to get back in your good graces."

We saddled our horses and rode out to check on the fence building.

"See that big outcropping of rocks?" Bernie pointed off in the distance. "That's what we needed the dynamite for."

"Why not build around them?"

"They're more on my property than his. I would lose so much land that I would have to cut a couple horses out of the herd."

"Cutting it that close, huh?"

"Yep, I need all the grass I can capture, and this fence is gonna do that for me," he said. "If I lose anymore grass, I might not survive til the end of the year."

We spent the afternoon watching the men work. At around six o'clock, we headed for the house. Sandra and Ruby had the table set and supper waiting for us.

"You missed dinner," Ruby said.

"When you own a horse ranch, you miss a lot of meals," Bernie said.

"Well, wash up and see what kind of damage you can do to this meatloaf?" Sandra carried the platter to the table.

We washed and sat down.

"You outdid yourself with this meal, Sandra," I said.

"Ruby made the meatloaf and the potatoes. In fact, she made pretty much the whole meal." Sandra smiled slyly. "She is going to make someone a good wife."

I looked at Ruby and she was grinning from ear to ear. What a beautiful sight she was.

"Well, Jubal, you want to try to catch a catnap before all the excitement?" Bernie asked.

"You men go ahead. We'll take care of the mess," Ruby said.

CHAPTER TWELVE

On my way up the stairs, I glanced back and saw Bernie heading for his room, then I looked at the dining room door and saw Ruby pass by carrying dishes. Once in my room, I splashed a little water on my face and lay down on the bed still dressed. I was dozing off when there was a soft knock on the door.

"Come in," I said, wiping my eyes.

The door opened and Ruby stepped inside wearing a thin dressing gown. "You want some company?"

"If you're offering the kind of company I think you are, then, you know the answer."

She untied the belt on her gown and let it fall at her feet. My breath caught in my chest, and I was at a loss for words. I had this beautiful woman standing in front of me with nothing on but a smile, and I couldn't say anything.

"Well, do you like what you see?" she asked.

"I . . . uh huh . . . you're beautiful."

~~~~~~~~~~~~

Later as we snuggled with her head cradled on my shoulder, we talked about what each of us wanted out of life. It was surprising how many of the things I wanted that she also wanted.
~~~~~~~~~~~~

"Can I ask why a beautiful woman like you has reached the age of twenty-six without getting married?"

"I was engaged for almost four years. We couldn't get married because both his parents were in bad health. When his father died, we felt sure we would be able to marry, but his mother didn't approve of me. I wasn't good enough for her son, so we held off. We were sure as ill as she was, that it wouldn't be long before she followed her husband in death. Our plans were to be married just as soon as she was gone, but she continued to hang on to life. Sometimes I think she did it to spite me. As I stated she didn't approve of me as a suitable mate for their son. Whatever illness his parents had must have been contagious, because Rudford died before his mother. The doctor tried to explain, but even he didn't have a satisfactory answer. Perhaps it was hereditary or something in their blood that caused the illness. His mother died shortly after he did. I, of course was heartbroken. I loved him very much. Then shortly after that, my parents were killed in that accident, like I told you. I kind of lost all desire for the opposite sex after that until now. I feel something special for you, Mr. Jubal Foxworth. Something I can't explain and even if I could explain, I'm not so sure I want to. Am I making any sense at all?"

"I feel the same about you, and I don't want to question or doubt those feelings I want to nurture them and help them to grow into something that no one or anything can tear apart. You are the woman I want to spend the rest of my life with.

"Are you going to give up being sheriff?"

I didn't immediately answer.

"You are, aren't you?"

"Ruby, I can't quit until they hire a replacement."

"How long will that take?"

"I'm not sure. You know the town needs a sheriff— one that knows what he's doing and can take care of any trouble that comes along. Right now, I'm that man. You can see that, can't you?"

"I'm not sure I can, Jubal. I would worry myself sick every day that you were doing your duty."

"I promise as soon as they hire a replacement I'll turn in my badge. I will, I promise. Please don't let this come between us. It's something that I cannot walk away from."

"Are you a man of your word, Jubal Foxworth? When you give your word, do you stand by it?"

"Absolutely," I said emphatically. "Grab my watch off the table there and tell me what time it is."

She leaned out of the bed dnd reached for my watch. I watched her body and thought to myself, *she's mine, all mine. I love her more than life itself.*

"It's a little after eleven," she said. "It's almost time, isn't it?"

"Yeah, I better get dressed." I leaned in and gave her another kiss.

I dressed and pulled my boots on, and she reached for me just as I was about to stand.

"Give me a kiss like you mean it," she said.

I wrapped my arms around her and pulled her close. Her lips touched mine gently, then I felt her tongue touching my lips. I opened mine just enough for her to gain entrance. *Now where did she learn to do that?* I asked myself. It was a glorious feeling when her tongue touched, and began twirling around mine.

"I've always wanted to try that," she said. "Some of my girlfriends told me about it. It was nice. Did you like it?"

"Enough to do it again, but not right now. I've got to get downstairs. Bernie will be waiting."

CHAPTER THIRTEEN

I gave her a kiss on the top of her head and left the room, taking the stairs two at a time. I was right, Bernie was waiting for me.

"I was beginning to worry that you weren't coming down," he said.

"I did think about staying up there, but I figured old Bernie needed me." I grinned.

"Did you leave your gun upstairs?" he asked. "You better get your head on straight before you go facing the trouble that's coming,"

"I'll be right back." I rushed up the stairs and into my room.

"Did you decide to come back and spend the rest of the night with me?" Ruby asked.

"I forgot my gun. I guess I had my mind on other things."

"You should maybe try to clear your head before you face those men that are coming?"

"That's exactly what Bernie told me."

I strapped on my gun and left again. *'Am I losing my mind? I better get it together pretty quick. What is it about love that makes you crazy? Maybe I better think real hard about staying sheriff. I wouldn't want to face a gunman and find out I forgot my gun.'*

"You think you're ready to do this?" Bernie asked.

"I'm ready."

We walked out to the barn, and the men were all waiting.

"You really think they'll show up?" Ned asked.

"If they do, what are we supposed to do?" Rowdy asked.

"Well, as the sheriff of this county, I reckon I need to ask them to give themselves up. If they don't, then it's gonna be extremely dangerous."

"What do you want us to do?" Drew asked. "Are we gonna stay in the barn and wait for them?"

"We need to catch them with the evidence in the wagon, so I figure all of us should wait behind the house until they get the wire in it."

"As soon as they have even a couple of rolls in the wagon, I'll shout out to them, then we'll find out if they want to obey the law. If not, well, you know how it goes."

"Alright," Bernie said. "Let's get behind the house and wait."

We hid and watched for half an hour before we saw the wagon pull up and stop in front of the barn. Two men were in the wagon with four astride horses. The men jumped down, while three of the others got off their horses. That left one man—for lookout, I suppose.

"Just rest easy, we don't want to spook them before they've done their dirty deed," I said.

The first rolls of wire were put on the wagon, and those two men were turning to go back inside when there was a loud explosion.

Luckily, we were located far enough away from the barn that the blast only shook us up. Renfro's men weren't that lucky, so it was going to be extremely hard to find enough of them to bury.

When the dust had settled, all that was left was a lot of debris and small crater in the ground where the barn had been.

"Get over there and see if there are any survivors," Bernie ordered.

"Couldn't nobody survive that, Bernie. Take a look. No wagon, no horses, no nothing, but a big hole in the ground," Ned said. "Best thing we can do for them is to cover up that hole and call it a grave."

"I reckon you're right," Bernie said. "Even the wire is destroyed. I don't guess we'll be building a fence until I can get more."

"Does that mean we're out of a job again?" Rowdy asked.

"No. I reckon I can find a place for you if you want to stay."

We all turned and saw Renfro coming into the yard. "I heard an explosion. What happened?"

"It seems you sent those men to die tonight," I said.

"What do you mean? I didn't send nobody no place. I don't know what you're talking about."

"It ain't gonna do you no good to deny it, Renfro. I saw them leave your place with a wagon earlier today," I told him.

"You ain't been no place around my spread. I'd have seen you."

"I was up on that little knoll just east of your place with my spy glass. I saw everything."

"What you plan on doing about it?" he asked.

"As sheriff, I'm going to arrest you," I said.

"What for?" he shouted. "You can't hold me responsible for what these men did."

"You want to try and talk me out of it, you're more than welcome to." I told him as my hand lingered over my .45.

"I ain't going to jail. If I have to shoot somebody, then that's what I'm gonna do." His hand reached for his pistol, but he didn't get it clear of the holster before he was lying in the dirt.

"Why'd he draw on you?" Drew asked. "You couldn't hold him in jail, could you?"

"No. There wasn't any way to prove he was responsible for what happened here," I said. "Some people are too hard headed for their own good."

I turned and saw both Ruby and Sandra running out the door.

"Boys." Bernie waved his arm. "Go on to bed and try to get a little rest, because tomorrow we're gonna clean up this mess and cover up the hole. Somebody get a blanket and cover Renfro's body. We'll let him join his friends in the morning."

"Are you alright," Ruby asked me.

"I'll be a lot better when you say you'll marry me. How about it? Will you marry me?" I asked.

"Sounds like a good idea," Bernie said. "We can have a double wedding, if it's okay with my bride to be."

"Sounds good to me," Sandra said.

"Yes. I'll marry you, Jubal Foxworth."

~~~~~~~~~~~~~~~~

Ruby wasn't just a stick of Dynamite, she was a powder keg of explosives.

I was definitely glad I hauled the dynamite from town . . . *BOTH THE BOXES AND THE WOMAN!*
~~~~~~~~~~~~~~~~

Books by J.C. Hulsey

Angel Falls, Texas
Velvet Sky, Arizona
Angry Orchard, Colorado
Clear Stone, Wyoming
Itching Tree, Idaho
Windy Butte, New Mexico
Devil's Dance, Dakota Territory
Redemption Road
Red Rose
Rebecca
The Concho Kid
Ugly Mugly
GUTSHOT
The Last Ride
The Old Man
The Pistol Preacher
Shortland
Dynamite
The Concho Kid
Dead Man's Gun
Does Nora Know
Doke Walker
Brothers
Satan's Refuge
Shadrack
The Brute
The Decision
The Greenhorn
The Gunfight
The Hangman